STRANGERS WE HAVE KNOWN

Strangers We Have Known

John Briscoe

San Francisco, California

ISBN-13: 978-1-7374947-2-0

"Washington Square" first appeared in the *San Francisco Chronicle* (February 26, 2021); "Land's End" first appeared in *Catamaran Literary Reader* (Volume 7, Issue 3, Fall 2019); "Oyster Shucker" was first published in the online journal *Eunoia Review* (Nov. 28, 2018); "Deaf Adder, Deaf Heaven" first appeared in *Marin Arts and Culture, 2017;* "Out Park Presidio" was published in *California Quarterly,* Volume 45, Number 2 (2019); "Common Prayer" first appeared in *California Quarterly,* Volume 45, Number 2 (2019); "To Mendocino" appeared in *The Antioch Review,* Vol. 70, Number 1 (Winter 2012); "The Changing Light of Sanderlings" appeared in *Northern California Super Lawyers 2021;* and "Conka" in the anthology, *Stories that Need to be Told* (Tuliptree Publishing, 2021). "Conka" is one of four finalists for the 2022 *Poetry International* Award.

The author wishes to express his gratitude to Joe Parisi of Chicago for reading the book in its manuscript form, offering invaluable thoughts and suggestions, and for his 25 years of tutelage, and close friendship.

Cover artwork by William Wolff

Author photo by Carol Sayers

San Francisco, California

For Carol

CONTENTS

IV.   Ineluctable Dimness of Being

V.   History, that "Poetic Endeavor"

I.

Caprices

CURLICUE

Writing *curlicue* in cursive
is swinging as a gibbon
through treetops,
swaying to be-bop
in bobby socks,
is drawing a curlicue
eight letters long.

GIBBONS, IN CLIMBS AND FALLS

Gibbons come not from Gabon,
Guinea, Ghana, or Guinea-Bissau,
not from Gambia, nor Cameroon,
but from Indonesia, Indochina,
and the Malay Peninsula.

Lacking tails they nonetheless dangle
from all observable appendages
from whatever limbs or branches,
swing, sway—then fling themselves
with tensile brawn and awing arms
branch to higher branch in timeless idleness,
from understory dwarf forests
to overstory crests in mindless wildness
thirty or more feet a fling and land
like swans on a pond, regally seated
in the crook of a branch or reclined upon
a verdant meadow of foliage, their aerie,
where they take their rest.

Then as though a stage direction flashed *Alarum!*
the gibbons rouse, rise, bound,
run, walk then leap
the slackened vines and sagging limbs
with feet and toes prehensile as high-wire artists.

They never slip but if they did we'd never know
for they recover with the grace and elegance
of Ginger Rogers quick-stepping back
from a Fred Astaire stomp on her instep
making all of it seem so utterly natural
and pointless as dance.

NOISES HOUSES MAKE

Noises houses make
across the abyssal plain of night
in an onslaught, of rain doubtless
pummeling the peeling clapboard siding
and the loosened window pane,
aren't heard at all until the outer racket

drops to that near stillness, and you wake.
Then they groan, snap rafters,
let slip a sixteen-foot-long ceiling joist,
drop a monkey wrench or iron prying bar
fluff like a heron, and flap away.
Whatever din they may that night, they make.
And all are noises houses
never make by day.

MISSIONS

Gray whale offshore Stinson Beach
breasting surf a foot beneath the sea
makes for the cape at Bolinas,
spouts once, twice, and breaches nearly
wholly out of the water, twists,
then flukes first slides
backflopping in,
rolls over bellydown,
turns, lobtails
and swims back toward
the place she had come from.

Above her snout and blowhole cormorants,
gulls, terns and pelicans shriek in frenzy,
dive in fury spearing missed and misflung fish.
Flocks of seagulls, hundreds in each, fly in
in formation, wheel, make for shore,
convene on a flat arena down the dunes
for some high covert purpose and, after a brief
convocation fly off in squadrons of twenty or so
to another parliamentary floor
a hundred yards upcoast.

Four sandpipers, a sanderling and one
long-legged child chase the receding surf,
then abruptly turn, squeal and race
fleeing its swishing uprush.

Tide floods
long past its time to ebb.
Time ebbs
even as it floods.

NIGHT FLIGHT

Low in the north northeast, and far
where there are no air fields near
a rumble rises, passes slow
miles overhead each night about this hour
of some time after midnight, two perhaps,
its pitch rising with its volume
and its apogee until it stalls
and after a long waking while restarts
its motors, or engines and resumes
southwesterly, its drone in diminuendo
though oddly still audible minutes later
when it must be far over the Pacific,
no apparent destination for its course
as there was no apparent origin.

ROOT CELLAR

Potatoes were blackin' in the root cellar
was all the man said to the immigration man
when asked at Ellis Island why
he had sailed without family in steerage across
the winter Atlantic from Ireland to America
in 1847.
That is what his grand-daughter, my grandmother,
told me he said. From then until he died
he never ate another potato,
only ramps, beets, turnips, carrots, lamb,
dairy and the other stuffs
the strangers had taken.
Two knifebladesful of butter
were dessert at Christmastime.

A home should have a root cellar, a place
I should have built years ago, and filled,
but instead I stored in paper notebooks
jottings of odd words come upon
like *turbary, alliaceous, frondescence,*
notes of obituaries, those little
biographies of strangers like Tom Turnipseed,
and stray phrases like "turnip snedder"
that long ago must have caught my eye or ear
enough that I tore them out, or scribbled
then ignored them. I can't say anyone
stole them from me.

Now and again though, one has grown eyes I see
like a potato, or sproutlings like an onion
or bulb of garlic, and is turning bitter, soft,
not good for eating, or keeping. I might as well
plant them then, and see what greens might shoot up,
what ones wither, which ones might store next fall,
which ones form the blight.

II.

Tongues

BIGFOOT

Newton discovered the ether.
Michelson and Morley discovered
the ether does not exist.

Sasquatch in Yurok is *Omah,*
in Hoopa, *Oh Mah,*
which one would think would tell us something.
But experts say there is no Sasquatch,
no Yeti, Santa, or ether either.

Why are things forever being
given names and then said not to be?
Why is there even a way
to say *not be*?

THE BIRDS OF BLETCHLEY PARK

The greater pewee is a passerine in the tyrant flycatcher group.

Just what the greater pewee natters
if she were about to pee
on a creamy clutch of the least grebe
is a mystery.

The common snipe's common name
for the common goldeneye
is a majesty of a riddle.

But how birds keep their downy dignity
when we heap on them the obloquy
of our witless names for them
is the alpha and omega of enigma.

Listen, at their sight of us, to their kreeches,
their squawks and skrills, their raucous cacophony.
Are they exchanging winter itineraries
or laughing at their giddy wicked names for us?

While Alan Turing's team was breaking
the Nazis' Enigma apparatus code,
the birds of Bletchley Park remained
staunchly defiant of decryption.

BERENICE

Jamais vu

A horse looked at, stared
at a long time in time becomes
like the word *horse* said
over and over aloud and over,
and over aloud again not more
but less horse and, in time's
fullness
fully unhorsed
as a dying fly's
morphosis
its eyes growing
more ever monstrous, wings
an anathereal green,
its so earthy buzz
unearthly

HEMLOCK

A pallid mash of root and crush
of purpled stems and sage-green leaves,
more stewed than steeped to a tea slew
Socrates, condemned for corrupting
young impressionable men of Athens
not with the usual seditious or seductive talk
but with a curious hubris of questions.
That hemlock, a shrub that grows to a small tree,
is an exotic in California, roaming rampant
the flood plains of rivers, flickering shade,
dappling air and overstory
like dogwood in spring.

No tea is brewed though from this, the native hemlock.
With the small tree it shares just the being
a tree, and the name expropriated for it.
It is a conifer that reaches heights of sequoias.
It lines the shores of the labyrinth of inlets
of Alaska's Alexander Archipelago,
flanks the glacier mouths of rubbled white ice,
traverses stiff-trunked up
the opaline Chilkat Mountains
    to their alpine line.
Its fir-like needles and dull dun of bark
don't tell the tree at all as well
as its crown, its leader does, drooped as though
it were too enfeebled, or shamed, named now as it is,
to stand erect among the near madrones
and alders, and its cousins the priapic
        spruce, and fir.

I ask an Athabaskan elder its aboriginal name.
He tells me his people have forgotten that,
but that its Athabaskan name is *yan*.
When I ask him he tells me *yan* means hemlock.

INTERIORITY COMPLEX

There is one spectacle grander than the sea, that is the sky;
there is one spectacle grander than the sky; that is the interior of the soul.
                                        —Victor Hugo, *Les Misérables.*

That may be but we, we have had our fill
of unrich, unstrange faux-intimate thoughts
spooled out in a jargon aphasia
by those to whom we must confess
our inability to disencrypt
the divinity to be found beneath
the din within the cacophony.
Not all colors seen in spring are art,
nor all fugacious thoughts or spattered words
poetry.

Do your minds teem with Dadaist verse
or ever see ten million shackled monkeys sentenced
to tap at typewriter keys for centuries
until a line, or maybe two, of Shakespeare,
Keats or Yeats appears?

To an aspiring young abstract painter
Picasso is reputed to have said,
    Draw me a horse that looks like a horse,
      and then I might look at your splotches and whorls.
To paraphrase the man, would one of you once
please write a tercet—or better, a sonnet
that looks, that scans like a sonnet, a sonnet
that doesn't sound like but *sounds* a horse.
Or a villanelle, a villanelle from hell
raging against this ever taking leave of light.
When you do, then we might try to read
your word-bucket heave.

THE MAN WHO FIRST WROTE IN PROSE

But for an almost forgettable Greek,
or possibly two,
we might still converse in verse perhaps,
singing as birds do instead
of chattering our jackbooted late-
Germanic cacophony.
He must have been a bit like me,
never picked for the archers or chariot-drivers.
The *demos* and the judges must not have liked
his rhyme or meter. So he shucked
their dactylic hexameter
and jived them with a first bop prosody,
a geographical treatise, his
Here I Am But Where Am I? first prose.

But for that man Anaximander
(it might have been that other fellow,
truth be told, Pherecydes of Syros)
perhaps we'd all be poets.
We would have no dreadful Fenimore Cooper,
no Edward Bulwer-Lytton but instead
a Shakespeare every other year
and many more Tennysons, Longfellows, and Lears.

Anaximander, or Pherecydes,
whoever was first to write in prose
unlike the conformist versists
of his day, was an early solipsist,
who believed in only *I ams,*
and not in dactyls and iambs.

HAIRCUT

Fly Fishing is the faint title impressed
in the faded cover of this battered book
buried under yesterday's obituaries
and Tuesday's sporting pages.
While waiting I read, "Evenings, duns emerge,"
and lay the book down.
Were these the words of Izaak Walton,
Thomas Best, the Miller in his Tale
or Beowulf himself, they would have set
the mind of J. R. R. Tolkien overteeming
with the palavers and plots of the Duns,
their wars against the middling Midges,
the gloatful Groats, the dreaded Wruins

and made him set aside what spread before him--
some manuscript on late Anglo-Saxon,
or early Middle English poetry --
to indulge his urge to reconnoiter such rare rents
into an ever more Middle Earth. Me,
I read the words once again stunned dull,
tongue numbed as though stuck to an icy streetlamp pole,
unable to make anything of duns,
managing only, "Above the ears."

PRESENT TENSE

All is so now
this moment.
No moment past,
no moment in the past
was ever nearly so now,
had nearly the vivor
(the noun form,
surely, of *vivid*)
of this one and present now.

Bird chatter is all, this now,
clearer than the dimming
of the din of voices on the pavement
of the just-past now,
now a park bench seat in winter sun,
now stray tingles of a lost orgasm,
now a sip of wine, now a slip
of the mooring lines of waking.

ET CARO VERBUM FACTUM EST

What was it you were
saying to yourself
before there were words?

Was it a wordless scene
from what would be Shakespeare?
Were you a mute voice
in some chorus Sophocles
found to be beyond his grasp?

Did you in that quietude
dream *pi*, in colors say
or silent notes, or *cogito ergo sum*?
Did you then reckon then that E
equals m times c squared?

What was the wordless language of thought—
spangles, ripples of light and shade,
or soundless music
of infinite and infinitesimal pitch?
Or was it palpable --
    the twitch of a phantom limb,
      a tinnitus whine at midnight,
        an aurora of phosphenes—are these
      its vestiges?

CY PRÈS PRÉCIS

Cy près, from old French,
is a legal 'doctrine'
the way religious writ is doctrine,
an incantation muttered
to aggrandize further the bearer
of the mitre, the wearer of the alb,
to ward off winds of apostasy,
to shelter its utterers
from the mistrals of misfits
who would storm and overthrow
the old order.

                    Cy près
is Proteus, the great Shape
Shifter of the Law, canting and twisting
words to mean whatever
they were never meant to mean.
Cy près is law's
                    most utmost Humpty Dumpty
who proclaimed the word "glory" to mean
"a fine knock-down argument." Doctrines
sigh and expire in the crash and smoke
of the bonfires of books.

                    Cy près looks
like *cyprès,* the French word for cypress,
a tree of true utility, for windbreak,
for fuel to kindle and stoke a fire
to warm a pot of mash, or stew,
to light a reading room,
to burn on iron andirons slow
to smoke and ash.

HERE AND NOW

The term for the unity of space and time was made to help explain Einstein's special theory of relativity.

—Encyclopedia Britannica

Time is an illusion.
—Albert Einstein

What here is there without its now?
Whatever now can possibly be
but a now that is here?

But if here is San Francisco now, how
can here be also Glasgow, Moscow,
Minsk or Krakow?

As here is also now
there must be too, for *then*, its *there*.
That is the logic *très extraordinaire*
of our meager grammar.

III.

Strangers We Have Known

LETTER TO RENÉ DESCARTES

Cogito ergo sum is your brief,
your proffered proof that you exist. It's a six-
syllable truncated syllogism,
its missing major premise lopped off
in the hope it goes unmissed
so that its breathtaking brevity
will beat for eternity
> with a drum sting,
>> the *DUN-duh-du DUN DUN DUN*
>> of uttermost authority.

In full, your syllogism is,

> *Qui cogitat est.*
> *Cogito*
> *ergo sum*

or in English,

> *He who thinks exists.*
> *I think,*
> *therefore I exist.*

What would your Aristotle say of your logic?
First he'd say you need to prove your shrilling
unsaid major premise, that he or she
who thinks exists. You, though, simply assume
that pesky matter away which is
the fallacy of begging the question,
what you in your prime would have called the sin
> of *petitio principii.*

Second he'd say that is also what you do
with your minor premise, the assertion *cogito,*
I think. For *I think* assumes that there's an I,
an I that is thinking, an I that *exists*,
and yet that is what you assert you are proving,

not assuming.

Third of course he'd ask, what is this thinking anyway?
You again assume what you ought to prove,
in this case that your dazzling mental phosphenes,
those fugacious fireflies flitting in your head
are *thinking.*

Come to think of it, what do you mean by *exist?*
Does arising at three to pee
establish that part of your case as well?
If so, this works also:

> *Mingo,*
> *ergo sum.*

Now what if you, whatever *you* is, or are,
are simply illuded into the thinking
there's a you who arises at three to pee?
And what if it happens you don't exist --
Si non sum, as you might write?
Who exactly is the *I*
in *If I don't exist*
who doesn't exist?

Lastly, don't you honestly prefer
a more mellifluous flow, say--

> *Cogito ego,*
> *Ergo sum?*

WASHINGTON SQUARE, FEBRUARY
In memory of Lawrence Ferlinghetti

Commandeering streets and strolling passersby,
the Green Street Mortuary Band,
those black-suited, dirge-blowing flâneurs seize all
of a falling noon in San Francisco's
North Beach, its Little Italy.
Cornets blare, saxophones wail,
trombones moan.
Tubas, and sousaphones bring low
whole blocks.   Kettle drums throb
as the band slow walks the hearse, and cortege.

Folks stand, doff hats, berets, bow heads.
Some weep, some pray. No one,
not any of the hundreds knows the dead—
a Chinese washerwoman, an old poet,
an Irish aunt, an elderly Black minister
or Italian butcher. No matter.
The custom, if it isn't ought to be--
    to mourn with the mourning.

OYSTER SHUCKER

Jacknimble fingers fly over and into
bushels of iced oysters, grab, grip, pierce
the thick ends with blade point, twist
and slide swift along slick silver mother
-of-pearl Sistine ceilings and shuck
as she distracts herself just
to glance to check for blood
   as a grubbing flicker flits
about her lettuce bed while Alice Murphy,
spinster-thin at ninety-one, sweeps her front stoop birdlike
the morning her spinster sister Irene dies
in their and their parents' house as if all
the neighborhood were coming for the wake already,
as fingers of the black Puerto Rican laborer
cut, bend and tie steel reinforcing bar,
or hands of the Kahnawake iron worker
swing a hoisted girder into its place
on the eighty-ninth *plein air* storey high
over Manhattan, fitting it tight
into its mate, pounding into paired holes bored
for two hundred years of no play
eight-inch cobalt-steel bolts, spinning nuts
onto the fine-machined bolt-end threads, wrenching them
fast, just to the stripping point.

The widowed Filipina oyster shucker
hoping each time it doesn't slip
plunges her knife in the hinge, twists, pries,
slides it against and along the upper shell
down each oyster, prays for Irene,
for Alice, for the Mohawk workers
and the so-black so-shunned Puerto Ricans,
and prays that if she slips she at least receives
the full stigmata.

BILLY HEBERT FIELD

Stockton, California, claims that it, not Holliston, Massachusetts, was the Mudville of "Casey at the Bat."

No one I know knows
who Billy Hebert was. Hebert--
pronounced not at all the way
it must once have been, *ay-bear,*
    but *hee-burt.*
Now the old field and scoreboard, the grandstand,
dugout, bases and sagging splintered bleachers
surely must be gone,
and Billy Hebert must lie in the ground.

A Stockton boy, he was a whippet
of a slugging second baseman for Stockton's Ports,
the Oakland Oaks, and the Merced Bears.
Lefty O'Doul, skipper of San Francisco's Seals
who found and coached the DiMaggio brothers
predicted Billy would be a star. He was.
Billy Hebert's Navy mates bore him home
when he was killed at twenty-two
in the Battle of Guadalcanal
in the fall of 1942.
Billy Hebert does lie in the ground,
in Golden Gate National Cemetery.

In 1951 a field that had been called Oak Park
was renamed Billy Hebert Field. Now
it has a shaded grandstand, metal bleachers,
proper sod and drainage, a major-league infield,
has yet to be renamed again,
and no one I know yet knows who
Billy Hebert was.

CRAZY BILLY

Why fire mesmerizes
mesmerizes. No flame
flickers as another,
none licks or forks
as any other after will.
What escapes, what
flies up the flue? Is it
what once was wood, or air,
or is it, or was it,
something other?

Old Crazy Billy
down there talking with the road
always bleeding, never hurting,
he'll reach in, he'll
snatch a flame for us.

He'll see.

I AM SO BORED

Harry St. John Bridger Philby, Arabist, naturalist, traitor and explorer, to his son, traitor Kim Philby, on the elder Philby's deathbed in Beirut, September 1960.

Rains fell before Arabia,
day upon day of steady sturdy rains
then fits, not flurries but squalls,
cloudbursts in tantrums
and then a spell, a slew, a spate of doldrums.
None, mind you, was superior to another.
All were equally dull.

Damn. Now there are crows,
sky-darkening flocks of crows,
raucous caucuses of crows
where there used to be crocuses,
desert owls, woodpeckers
and my partridge-- no crows then,
only shrikes and whoopoes,
boobies, bulbuls and some other
bore of a bird.

IAGO'S CREED

Yes, I believe in God, who has created me like himself, cruel and vile
—Arrigo Boito, Verdi's *Otello*

Don Thackeray, or Thackrey may have been his name,
the UPI reporter fifty years ago
who covered the federal courts in San Francisco.
He hung out evenings in Rocca's bar on Golden Gate
with the U.S. Attorney and FBI guys,
and they were all guys then, and with me.
One night he talked of being a young writer
stumbling upon unfamiliar words
especially as a police-beat reporter,
and told of a two-syllable villain
worse than a robber, worse than a murderer,
who was always, oddly, a child.
He never once, he leaned toward to tell me,
came upon a police-blotter entry
for an adult mole-ster.

Child mole-sters have gotten a pass perhaps
in the way we speak or write of their crimes.
We have a sordid penchant for euphemism.
We say they "abuse" children which today
describes a father who withholds dessert
from a son who refuses to eat dinner
or curses his mother.
Or we say they "molest" children,
using the word the environmental police
use to render criminal whatever
might annoy an animal that can be found
on *their* lists of protected species.
We're squeamish about writing plainly
what these people really do to kids
but if we did, if we wrote of their forced
diddling, fondling, and worse,
would our indignation rise,
would would-be mole-sters be deterred

by any heightened shame?

Of all the "abusers" of children, so called,
Catholic priests may be the purest fiends,
practicing a villainy deserving of
its own circle so close in Hell to Satan
that his icy breath freezes their eyes agape
so they must watch Ugolino gnaw
on Ruggieri's skull eternally
before they are flogged to take their turns
on each other's jawbones, and ossicles.
For their sins are compounded manyfold
by what they taught the children all those years--
that all sex, even a slight lingering
of a hand upon one's own, never mind
another's nether parts is wrong except
only in the marriage bed, and only then
when for the purpose of procreation.
And what is more the least transgression
of this rule of God is a mortal sin,
a sin of a grievousness equal to murder,
equal to the murder of six million people,
a sin that condemns the sinner to plunge
into Hell for all eternity, a sin
only a priest can expunge.

BEVERLY'S DAUGHTER

Your father's father was an Okie, someone said.
Your mother maybe too for all I knew
but she was beautiful and I, a boy,
was not supposed to notice I suppose
a distant older cousin's wife.
Your father was good looking too
in that sullen James Dean way.
He'd come over the house his T-shirt torn,
blood dripping from his nose or mouth, or both
and had been drinking, I figured later.
I'd hang out at the curb by his hot rod
while he cried before the family elder,
my impassive dark-skinned father wearing suit and tie.
Your father would leave his hotrod running, radio on
tuned to a station playing Hank Williams—

> *Did you ever see a robin weep*
> *when leaves begin to die? . . .*

> *Why can't I free your doubtful mind,*
> *and melt your cold, cold heart . . .*

> *Your cheatin' heart*
> *will tell on you . . .*

I never did know what to make
of any of it.

GIVING THE NOOSE THE SLIP

The man who had been a long time dead
tells his friend's Christmas party every year
what death is. Death is light, a dazzling white.
St. Peter does stand by those gates, he tells
insistently, which truth to tell are pearlescent,
not pearly. He is earnest and his story
though consistent, is never word for word.

He might remember one year what
one angel said to him, what St. Peter joked
another time, but always what that light was like.
Raising his trembling glass to toast our host,
with a finger that always misses at first
he taps his canted, dropping head,
says he is glad to be with us this day,
but truth be told he'd rather he were there instead.

Sweetwater
Nat Clifton, 1922-1990

1.

Only a Checker Marathon could have held that man
driving the overlarge yellow taxicab I hailed
in a hail-and-rain Chicago maelstrom
looking to make an eastbound flight, or westbound
forty years ago late one August afternoon.
Downtown he wove through the city's work crews
clearing sewers and storm drains, checking pumps
and took all the right side streets through South Side rush hour
beginning a new story every three or four blocks
of jazz joints, gone ones, really gone ones,
rib shacks, bars, long-ago prize fights,
the real Sugar Ray, Paul Robeson, Clay,
and he got me to Midway on time.

When about the fifth story I saw a jersey
of the Harlem Globetrotters hanging snug
on a young man in a faded color snapshot
Scotch-taped over a gash in the dashboard
I recognized the driver, who'd told me his name
was Nat. He was Sweetwater,
the man many said broke the color barrier
in American professional basketball
(the NBA, that is; the Globetrotters
didn't count). But he had no photo of himself,
he told me, in the uptown uniform
of the New York Knickerbockers,
the NBA team he later played for
when the league was finally, because of him,
integrated. All soft exuberance, he was even
more endless stories then, of Chicago, jazzmen,
actors, politicians and ballplayers—
Bebo Valdes, more Paul Robeson,
Ernie Banks, Minnie Miñoso, Goose Tatum--
and he did get me to Midway on time

and it was only later, in the air
that I remembered I remembered none of them.

He did get me to Midway, just in time
for my flight to LaGuardia, or Salt Lake.
I ran through the airport as I would then, and boarded the flight
though at thirty-thousand feet I wished he had been late
or that I had had the wit to ask him to turn back
so I could have hired him to drive me
all over Chicago, along the lake shore,
under the El and around the Loop all night
just to listen to him ever more.
Not for nothing was he called Sweetwater.
That ride would have to be another day.

2.

But as way leads on to way
I never came back for that taxi ride,
and I read somewhere that Sweetwater died.
Bud Palmer-- Sweetwater's Hollywood-born
white teammate, inventor of the jump shot
some said, his roommate when the Knicks
were on the road, say in St. Louis where Blacks
were unwelcome-- Palmer's died too now,
same year as Mandela, and Bebo.
From the obituaries I gather
Palmer was a buddy, a sort of Pee Wee Reese
to Sweetwater's Jackie Robinson.

The forty last blocks to Midway
like storm clouds gather in memory.
The cloudbursts pass, or rather pause.
Drop inlets clog, or the lake has risen too high.
The South Side squats in squalid water
to its curb tops, here and there overtopping
its sidewalks to its stoop fronts and down
into basement bedrooms, and kitchens.
Young men and old, women long past sullen

emerge from rows of clapboard buildings slow,
lean against peeling walls and grime and stand
under faltering street lamps dimming in the dusk.
No city work crews are arriving here.
No Bud Palmer, no PeeWee Reese stands near.
Not far away, though, stand black-suited men,
dead men with names of Bull, Bilbo, Wallace
and Faubus, glower over the spreading sheen
of standing bitter water.

CONKA
Emelia Serrano Briscoe, b. circa 1896, d. 1973

When all the others were away at mass
it was like that with me too.
I stayed home with her and her floured hands
and hair and apron. From the icebox
in the screened-in pantry she carried in plates
of dough balls she had made the day before
of flour, *manteca*, water and salt,
each the size of my little fist.
Taking the top ball from the pyramid
she'd flatten it with the heels of her palms
then fingers working beneath the dough, thumbs
on top, begin to whirl a widening disc
much as I had seen the Italian cooks do
with two big hairy hands and much more dough
then would stop mid-spin and ask me in Spanish,
What is a mouse when it spins?
before handing me a dough ball to try myself.
She would guide my little fingers but I,
I think now, could never get the hang of it.
Like a cook uncurdling a broken sauce
she'd repair my torn and tattered tortilla,
cook it on the griddle side of the stove,
a Wedgewood wood-burning stove and tell me I had made it.
She'd sizzle lard in a skillet to scramble eggs
with chopped calves' brains and maybe
she'd make hot chocolate--

> *Sesos con huevos, con tortillas y--*
> *acaso, tal vez, quizas, --*
> *chocolate caliente.*

Come to think of it she never sat down
to eat with me, and rarely then with others.
She only cooked for and served me, and cleaned
after me, and told me stories the while
of her husband, my grandfather murdered

by a stranger just for his police badge
when she was only twenty with four sons,
of my father and his three younger brothers,
of her mother Trinidad, a singer
and bar dancer, and her father Fernando,
the woodcarver of Old St. Mary's Church
in Phoenix, Arizona Territory,
who was also a saloon keeper
who could not enter the saloon he owned
because his kind was not allowed in a bar
anywhere in White Man's Country
anywhere in the country.

That's how I know
what little I know of her.
That's how I know
what little I know.

IV.

Ineluctable Dimness of Being

EXISTENCE

How God Became

Not trying at all, in the oddest places
we find faces--
in the gnarled bark of burls,
in the spirals, veins and whorls
of marble, in clouds.
So why would we not try
to find a face in what we think is this?

DORVEILLE

Coyotes bay, now howl
like morning sleet, like winds
that sweep down from the high jagging ridge,
whine past the hidden den, shrill
in the fishtail slipstreams of scree falls
through the shut night window to wail across
the steppes of these heaved
bedclothes.

Or is it your breathing,
slightly wheezing,
that is mourning so baleful,
so full of dolor?

MY I AND MY CASTAWAY ME

What if my I and my castaway me
were to get greatly along?
Would they or could
they marry?
Is one of them man
and the other a woman
or does it not matter
   at all?

Were they to marry
would they merge and if so
which one
like an elf
would un-
appear?
Which one would not, and whatever would happen
to that other fine soul,
   myself?

FIRST PERSON

I met myself in town today,
we hadn't seen each other, Lord—
    years out of time.
I hadn't changed much but he,
he had. The paunch
and gray of course, but more
his stillness.
It was as though he —no,
he was in fact unblinking,
a hard thing to do, and when he spoke
he didn't gesture with his hands at all.
They and his long arms
hung at his side stock-still.
He was gentle, and quietly arrayed.
He somehow drew me to him.

I had always had my preference, I.
I had never cared much for me nor paid
much mind at all to this fellow.
Now, though,
I think he's most favored.

SUCH I

Such a sense of I suffuses
this daybreak, this day, this bird-beak day.
Robins and starlings fly in, roost, boast
in arias Puccini would wish
he had composed. A breeze sighs,
a live oak sways, then groans in winds
that wail in moans from a hell
Wagner hadn't the wit to hear, or score,
though my I hears.

Mute moon, still stars
in firmaments of your own chaos,
do your synapses flit and snap?
Do your numberless atoms dream as one
like mine? Do you think things so sublime
that we can never divine but only bare
our awe before you? Surely not, for if you did
you would be the I supreme, the I
over all and no one, nor no other thing
can have such a sense of I as I.

DODDERING TOWARD CREDO

Nessun Dorma soaring
from Pavarotti's core

     a glimpse
through glass
  of Rodin's "The Kiss"

     last squalls of a passed typhoon
  silhouetted at the horizon by a sunset that irradiates
    all the galleries and vault of sky
      and the troughs and crests of the Philippine Sea below--

 these grace motes of awe
must be so like what
 a believing in God must be like, so
   like a believing in God
     they may be a believing in God.

WAKE

Voices murmur along the bare-floor corridors,
their moth-chewed runners rolled and stowed away,
mumble hushed and sidelong in huddled doorways,
chatter in one corner of the anteroom,
in the walnut-wainscoted side room
where antimacassars drape the worn backs
of burgundy mohair chairs,
and in the doilied, lily-scented parlor where she lies
swathed in white linen in her open coffin
laid on a table the undertaker brought,
her altar, for now.

The whisper, banter and clamor of talk
collide with clatter of plates, saucers, platters,
the *tink tink* of silverware, the clangor of pots
brought down from upper pantry shelves and everywhere
the clinking of bottlenecks rapping rims
of chipped and mismatched Waterford crystal stemware
washed, dried and polished for the first time in years.
All pound out an *ostinato,* a ground bass pierced
with bursts of shrieks, gasps, and giddy laughs
that peal, fade, heave and subside, a chorus of hearts
in arrhythmia

                that in hours yields
to more orderly din, no
voices in hubbub, only a hiss,
trickle, then running of water pouring
from faucet into pitted porcelain sink
to rinse, wash and rinse again the glasses,
forks, knives, dishes and, in a softer patter,
the setting down of everything on towels
that another grandmother cut and hemmed
from Sperry flour sacks.

In bed at last, a brief near noiselessness
as of a bomb blast far away arrives
before the cicada hiss of silence descends
when the curtain of sleep rises
and a new din, of old dreams
resumes its stomp and blare
on that creaking firetrap stage.
Soon enough though, even that
ceaseless racket will end.

UPPER STORY

As usual it is an upper story,
a hidden or forgotten upper story, one
far above the basement of origin,
one or several flights of stairs above
the floor that all had thought the uppermost.
And as usual its reprises surprise
the dreamer, who is almost always you
though a stranger or ancestor will do.
And the dreamer is often too the actor
watched and listened to
by the dreamer.
Often as not, though
the dreamer is you, only as actor,
or you only as the unseen observer.
protector perhaps,
the one who can pull the emergency cord
at the imminence of death of the actor who
intimately familiar with the lower floors
climbs a vined-over staircase to come upon
a place only now recalled
from prior dreams, or times.

Its walls, tall panels of Brazilian walnut,
its ceilings box-beamed in the same wood,
silk rugs of red and ivory medallions
bound around by fields of copper abrash
sprawl its floors, and gilt-framed portraits
of no known persons hang crooked on its walls,
staring askew. A large bay window
looks out on a long bay curving what
may be northerly, to a cape that is crowned
with a lighthouse flashing fourteen seconds.
Four oarsmen in a dory row across,
into and through the sea's crisscrossing currents
toward a surging surf and shore
they never reach.

A grand piano sits
in one of the room's many corners.
No one plays it. No one ever has.
A writing desk stands against a bare wall,
its reading lamp lit.
No one ever writes at it but on it
on sheets of what all know, or whisper
is foolscap, is writing that not one of you
can make out.

TO MENDOCINO

This storm, its thunder its
barrage of rain bombard
the coast road and car
all the night ride here.

Morning
all stills.
Skies clear
when chaparral on the bluff top teems
when wrens flit
in blackberry hedges
        and coyote bush,
when red-shouldered blackbirds fly
pine top to cypress crown
harassing crows unalarmed until
a late lost gust upends them
mid-flight. The sea
still seethes.
It rises and pounds this jut, this
taunting promontory
of the calving continent,
recedes,
        heaves.

Dreams last evening were usual
but vivider, were humdrum things done up
in high wit and horror.
Dreams here usually are.
I prefer the shore.
It makes a mimicry,
a grotesquerie
of the interior.

TWO ROCK CEMETERY

Weatherwhite gravestones
seem to tell, when not near
and in a right light, not
this shadow of a scudding cloud
flickering with the wheelings
of raptors overhead,
dates of birth and death
and names perhaps,
though now they appear
to be bleached white cypress stumps
scattered among six survivors
green at their tops that droop
like western hemlocks,
their roots splayed over plots
long untended, telling nothing
of their talons' hold.

FINAL ANOINTING

Agnus Dei, qui tollis peccata mundi,
  miserere nobis . . .
dona nobis pacem.

Incense burnt and wafted,
last rites uttered, the priest departed,
a last lustful thought, a mortally sinful
lustful thought
flickers in on onionskin wings,
alights on its jutting chin,
splays a promiscuous orificial grin
and you, ever superstitious
of Satan's ever surreptitious wiles
expire.

DEAD AT LAST

Yeats said, *To those who see spirits, human skin*
For a long time afterwards appears most coarse.
                            --Seamus Heaney

Dead, dead at last.
Jailer, cellmate, and cell
all in one incarnate form, you're soon dead
and I may be away again
(though I need to relearn how to waft about

without having you to drag along).
A last heaved breath, a sigh, a quiver,
two uncinematic rattles
and you release me.

Now all that is left is for me to rise
and hover over you, where I will be seen
only by entering children
and the women body washers
and tarry only long enough until
I have seen them, and seen
and marveled how your skin is,
the raiment, or *deshabillement*
of my former so-called temple, and be away,
like the sons of the wife of Usher's Well
at daybreak.

Will I in the age to come learn how
to animate the dreams of my children
as I suspect my long-late father did mine,
or will I merely script, choreograph
and direct more follies of the absurd,
the usual fare of dreaming
whether asleep or awake?

WHEN WE ARE OLD AND ONLY SOULS

When we are old and only souls
standing awkwardly around

will we stand stranded by the sides of roads
that once rode the crowns of banks
of the Ganges, or Yellow River,
or switchbacked up the Khyber Pass,
    or to Machu Picchu?
Will we mill about in vacant railway stations
in some pre-war Budapest, Prague, or Minsk
that through old coal smoke still huff and echo

off vaulting windows of lead-glass panes cracked and grimed,
waiting as ever more of us arrive
none ever turning to speak, to show a face,
and will the anonymity of facelessness
be solace?
                    Sure with the comfort of no faces
we will stand there stilling
until our spindrift beings,
ashen as that smoke, stir, lift aloft, and waft
braiding up through steel beams and columns
to the soaring iron arches
converging at the ceiling's apex,
converging and compressing there in one
infinitesimal oblivion
for one moment --
As the whole station empties,
we descend to stand, alone on the platform.
The eleven fifty-five arrives, and we
rebegin again.

V.

History, That Poetic Endeavor

—Lawrence Ferlinghetti

THE DEATH OF LIGHT VERSE, MAY 1, 1919

I never saw a Purple Cow,
I never hope to see one;
But I can tell you, anyhow,
I'd rather see than be one.

> --Gelett Burgess, in *The Lark,* 1895

World War One, the Great War, the War
to End All Wars killed sixteen million people,
maimed as many more and made mad
the King of England, the Kaiser and the Czar, all
cousins, grandsons by birth or by marriage
of Great Britain's Queen Victoria.
After Armistice, at the peace conference,
furniture in the Palace of Versailles
so distressed America's President Woodrow Wilson
that he began moving pieces around with commentary
that might have been scripted by Artemus Ward, or
    Samuel Clemens
on clashing reds and greens and, fixating on one chair,
called down the little poem published in San Francisco
twenty-four years earlier that most Americans
had read or heard and many, like Wilson,
knew by heart. Said Wilson,

> *Here is a big purpose, high-backed covered chair,*
> *which is like the Purple Cow, strayed off to itself,*
> *and it is placed where the light shines on it too brightly--*

Wilson maundered on, then sat himself
on the tucked plush upholstery of the Purple Cow,
scrawled payment schedules for German reparations, arose
and wandered dazed into the Hall of Mirrors,
meandered the colonnaded portico
of the Grand Trianon, shuffled through
the *orangeries* to the gardens down
to Saturn's Fountain and into his own

new mind for the rest of his days,
making company with the Kaiser, King and Czar.

   Ogden Nash and Dorothy Parker
kept the flame aflicker awhile but Wilson's rant
might have been the first snuff
of the nation's love of little sense and
nonsense in verse. Soon
no respectable magazine
would publish a Burgess lark of a poem,
no Edward Lear limerick,
no Lewis Carroll Jabberwocky.

   Had, instead of Wilson,
William Howard Taft gone daft
chattering from the same light verse
we might all be off less worse.

NOW APPEARING AT THE MUSEUM OF LONDON, THE WHITECHAPEL FATBERG

Ἴδμεν γάϱ τοι πάνθ', ὅσ 'ἐνι Τϱοίη
(*We know all the things that belong to Troy*).

Whirling and whorling in a widening gyre
the Great Pacific Garbage Patch, just as a black hole
traps light, entrains in its impassive maelstrom
herring, sardines, hake, whales and porpoise,
albatross, petrels, lost cormorants and gulls,
sucks all into its maw and down
its descending abyssal wake.
So fecund, so otherly immortal,
it will not only survive but in
this global warming thrive, will
with another atomic holocaust
mutate only more robust.

Coleridge might have told Sir Humphry Davy
science ought well to study what method
lies back of the mad genius of Londoners
who had the wit to emulsify
their household rubbish, condoms and excrement
with rancid cooking fat, motor oil and other congealants
to bind all into a museum piece of a cake nine hundred feet long,
of one hundred thirty tons displacement, the last remaining bit of
which,
salvaged from the cavernous sewers of London near Whitechapel,
reposes on display nearby other high-water marks of high
civilization--treasures looted from the graves of Pharaohs,
jewels heisted during the British Raj,
the Benin Bronzes and, most prized,
the masterpieces of Phydias
chiseled, hammered and pried from the friezes
and pediments of the Parthenon then
spirited out of their land by an earl,
of Elgin, to London
where the Fatberg, gift of millions of Londoners,

is the one only grandly wrought,
literally *magnificent*,
unstolen object.

EARTH, IN BRIEF
Meditation on a beach, Playa Sisal, Yucatán

1

Fourteen billion years ago the Big Bang stirred
what wasn't there and thus began the universe,
the one we know although the word itself
suggests that there's just one. What was there before,
or here perhaps, is a puzzle of another plane.
Then came the epochs, the Planck, the Quark, the Hedron,
the Grand Unification and others all
crammed into just the first second
of our universe's life, followed by
longer ones, like the Photon Epoch
which lasted three hundred and seventy thousand years.
In more and more time, in ten billion years
our Earth began to coalesce
as a swarm of gasses wobbling about
a sinuous, wavery axis
until it cooled, steadied, formed oceans,
and spawned life.

2

In very later history came a day
a mere some sixty million years ago
when an errant comet or moon struck Earth
here, or near here, at Chicxulub,
with the force of a billion Hiroshima bombs.
The Chicxulub Impactor, its given name,
destroyed three-fourths of life on Earth,
making that much easier Darwin's job.
Dinosaurs lumbered and roared their last,
but from that irruption, in the fullness of time
in our own breech birth we too oozed forth, butt first.

Messier Eighty-Seven,
a galaxy appearing to be
in the constellation Virgo, holds a black hole
sixty million light years away from us
that just sat for its portrait, the first ever from-Earth
portrait of any black hole in fact, though what we really see
is its dark countenance of sixty million years ago,
about the time that heavenly Impactor
slammed into the Yucatán. As we take its,
is it also taking our picture,
capturing the moment that moonlet struck Earth, here?

The name of the black hole is *Powehi*,
which means unending adorned dark creation
from the Hawaiian creation chant *Kumulipo*,
first heard by Captain Cook and his syphilitic men
in 1779. Coupling wanton
with the native women, the men
dated the chant from their first hearing it.

3

In Lahaina, Cancun, on the Isle of Man,
all around the Earth, eight billion *I*'s of us,
we clotted clusters of atoms, we *I's,*
apprehend profundities such as now,
here, time to sleep, rise, to piss, eat, fuck,
most of the sequence of a chowder recipe,
and Pythagoras's Theorem.
The greatest of these *I*'s might compose
Nessun Dorma, might write

> *To be or not to be,* . . . or
> *Arma virumque cano . . .,*

or understand $E = mc^2$.

Being so much larger an assemblage of atoms,
what greater thoughts Powehi must ponder
or Messier Eighty-Seven of which
Powehi is but the navel, the omphalos.
Do they share a wry *New Yorker* sense of humor
as they watch our *Erda*, our Earth,
as that asteroid crashes into Chicxulub
when we were still so many millions of years away
from learning to slither and in time crawl
among a whole new palette of plants
and menagerie of beasts?

Or have they conquered the irksome slowness of light
and watch us in real time
as we scald our planet, acidify its seas,
foul its skies with ash and soot as though
a comet had again collided here,
all in a ritual preparation
for destroying life on Earth for once and all
ourselves this time?

4

Here, on the northwest cusp of Yucatán,
across from Playa Chac Mool, from Cancun
we sip *Añejo*, stare
at flashes of flying fish,
watch sunsets burst spectacular as atomic blasts
over Kwajalein, Eniwetok, Bikini Atoll,
over Moscow, Beijing, Seoul,
over the Near East, Far East, McMurdo,
over San Francisco, over Michoacán.

STANLEY CUP RIOTS, VANCOUVER, 2011

The Nika Riots in Constantinople erupted in January, 532 CE when unhappy fans of the Greens, which were sporting teams, turned into violent mobs. The mobs burned half the city, including the Hagia Sophia, and stormed the palace of Emperor Justinian. Justinian, cowering, planned his abdication. His wife Theodora, recently retired as a live-sex performer who had caught her future husband's eye, stiffened his spine with a scold that will stand for the ages. Justinian thereupon had 30,000 of the rioters slaughtered in the Hippodrome alone, put down the riots, and went on to do great things. He became, in fact, Justinian the Great. And, for good measure, a saint.

Everyone in town the next morning said *they*
were not from here, but from *the valley*,
as they, and everyone everywhere swept glass and hauled trash
from the riots of the night before that started
before Vancouver even lost the hockey game,
to Boston or someone.
A foreigner, I didn't understand at first
until I realized they meant the *Okanagan* Valley.
For a moment I'd thought that this was one long way
for those bad boys of that other valley
to come.

Those Okanagan boys broke and burned a bunch that night
but truth be told they were laughable street fighters,
and they didn't manage to kill a soul.
Their Empress back in London didn't blink,
didn't flinch, didn't once think
of abdicating.

The First Nations people, the Syilx,
say their first people in the valley
were not at all that way.
They would tolerate a theft of land,
a burning of a village, a rape,
a massacre here and there
without raising nearly such a fuss.

SAY HER NAME SOFTLY

Political enemies murdered Tiberius Gracchus in 133 BC. The murder was the first political bloodshed in the nearly four hundred years of the Roman Republic. The same enemies twelve years later assassinated Tiberius's brother and two hundred and fifty of his allies. After many more assassinations, in fewer than a hundred years more, the Roman Republic lay dead.

They will kill her.
They will kill her
surely as they killed Kennedy,
surely as they killed King, Christ, Kennedy,
as they killed Lincoln, and King's own mother,
as they killed King's own mother in her own church,
King's own mother in her own husband's church,
King's own mother in her own son's church.
They will kill her.
They will kill her one day.

In moldering Oklahoma grange halls,
in northern Wisconsin cattle barns, and churches,
in bars off dust-deviled Bakersfield crossroads,
in rib joints along Atlanta boulevards across
from massage spas they plot, plan, script,
they rehearse her assassination.
In the solemn chamber of the Senate,
in the solemn chamber of the House of Representatives,
they plot, plan, script, and rehearse.
They are the unmarked descendants,
the baseborn offspring of Booth, Oswald, Ray,
of Caligula, of Cain.
Bred by their fathers and sisters to kill
they and their litters live to kill and live
to kill the best the rest
of the race brings forth.

Speak her name seldom,
say it soft.
Watch over

her, watch over
her home for her.
And when they have come for her
we say we are her,
we draw the fire meant for her,
we help place the noose around
our own necks.
Keep her alive
as long as we can.
For they will kill her,
they will kill her surely
one day.

DEAF ADDER, DEAF HEAVEN

Venom hisses
in *Jewess,* in *Negress,*
but it cannot ooze
from innate sounds of the words.
It must lurk in the sneering sibilant way
this woman chooses to
enunciate them.

Then again *mimsy, slithy toves*
and every child's favorite *borogoves*
made us giggle long before Humpty Dumpty
told Alice what they meant.
For that matter if *borborygmus*
were redefined to mean Armageddon
we still would titter at its silly sound
I suspect.

My grandmother, who raised me, suckled me
she told me, would have forbidden me to dwell
even a day in this place, Squaw Valley,
squaw being the most mocking caw of *kooni,* crow,
a word crueler than *nigger,* crueler
than the unutterable
the for-this-you-fight-Son *D* word,
for if I were bad she would say, *I will take you*
to Place Where They Burnt the Digger.

My eyes flit up one granite cliff, alight
on a saddle on its east, drop down its draw
to a high spring that runs and falls and feeds Squaw Creek
feet from me where the August grasses part
fast as a bobcat's prowl, and flatten
silent. A snake I cannot see must be
sidewinding by the bank, down the valley
to the Truckee.
A raven croaks. A crow
squawks retort.

I grope, dig hard
but cannot hear her hurt.

VI.

One Touch of Nature

OUT PARK PRESIDIO

Evening soon will spill across the milkened sky.
I pause, and take my coat, and leave to walk
out the city's blocks and greens, west along
its long boulevards and streets, speaking but little
and soft, and often mute,
listening intent to you
who aren't there,
turn into avenues
of a certain shadow, green or yellow avenues
that lead to Clement, or California Street
or, north from Lake Street, into gray
vestiges of avenues that stop
at the Presidio or enter Seacliff and wend
into the road that winds through Lincoln Park and ends
at the Palace of the Legion of Honor
and Auguste Rodin's *The Thinker* glistening
in the lifting mist. Where is his
The Kiss? I forget.

      I walk on high
      above the Golden Gate
   on the buckled ruins of the cliff road
to Land's End and look to sea to see
what is never there, to see what millions
of people have stared to see, looking
for what they also did not know.

Do we like the carlin wife of Usher's Well
look for sons lost long ago at sea?
Do we look for an empty bobbing dory,
or only for whatever
may not be there?

COMMON PRAYER, SUTRO HEIGHTS

Winds wave and sway
cypresses, whisper
matins.

Streetcar clangor, iron rumble
are carillon and organ bass,
an Angelus.

The rush of surf
hushes
the hummed vespers.

All this will
or was perhaps.

LAND'S END
Near Cape Mendocino

Near sunset cows low, somewhere --
there, the far pasture near
where oaks, madrones and pines appear
to graze the ridge, and browse down its slope
this way, fifteen in all perhaps,
five adults, brown spotted white, with small dun horns.
Lowing again, in
no discernible chorus
they shamble off with some of the young
to some place, perhaps to sleep.

The low salmon sun
slips beneath the sea.
Indigo washes
all the sea's phosphorescence.
and all but the most western sky.

Five calves stay back, playing late
this day's end, with the purposeless energy
of bounding fawns, gamboling and butting heads
right in the paths of three oncoming heedless steers
and a cow returning, black spotted now,
equally with no reason.

RIVER NAMES

1

Rivers meander America's East,
roam and wander loamy banks, flow slow
past low limestone walls. Their names loll also
through all our early allegories, those
of Hawthorne, Thoreau, Fenimore Cooper
and Clemens— the Concord and the Charles,
the Susquehanna, Ohio, Hudson,
the Mississippi and the Allegheny.

Names of rivers in the West -- the Mad, the Pit,
the Snake and Eel—flit, dart and sniggle
as their rivers grind, abrade and blast
their granite walls to boulders, scree and grit,
as they rive the gorges and canyons where
we wait through surge and crash of water onto rock
to strain to listen in the ebb through the din
of English, Spanish, and Yurok names
for the names coyote, deer and bear, crow,
eagle, and osprey know for them but most
for their own names, maybe never sounded
but by them.

2

What matter our or their
or any other names?
What can Modoc, Yurok
or Wailaki names tell,
and why do we want to know?
The Eel was *Taanchow* to the Cahto,
Wyat to the Wiyot.
When Josiah Gregg had gone, or became
or made himself mad, other half-mad white men
named a river, maybe it was the Lasik,
maybe the Whilkut, the Mad in his honor

and in heady celebration those men then
slaughtered all the local tribes.
History jotted down the incident
all in American English,
as the Bald Hills War. Ospreys and eagles,
wary of the fetid carcasses, left them
to the wolves, buzzards, and beetles.

What does the osprey
call otter, call salmon, call
a breaching or straying orca?
What does the eagle call osprey, call
Mount Lassen, what does Lassen call Mount Shasta
and what did they all call the mighty Sacramento,
the Nile of California, before we poured
a concrete embolus six hundred feet high
into the narrowest artery
of its aorta?

LATE DECEMBER

Sun, the old same sun
lies low, almost below
its south. Cows
begin to low, begin
to wander home.
The old stallion,
once the steed, later, for a time
the stud, shambles
slow towards the trough
corral and barn
halt, stops to rest
and look his chestnut eyes at me
as if saying something sounding like
 you too, *now.*

MARLIN FISHING
The Marianas Islands

Deck hands grunt in Chamorro,
the language their ancestors muttered
when conquerors from the Philippines,
Polynesia and Spain,
America, Japan and America again
dropped sail.
An equatorial Pacific tongue,
its mutterings sound
like a Celtic onomatopoeia.

Only a bonita, a small tuna,
has been caught, and a few
flying fishes that landed,
adventitiously, in the boat.
The typhoon, a day out, has passed to the north
but the squalls in its wake have borne down on us the afternoon
thundering like the shelling of Mindanao

or the bombing of Ujelang.
The rumble of thunder,
diesel and screw, the snap of lines, the thwack
of fishes writhing on the yawl's teak deck
are all another guttural babble
straining with the yards and sails to be heard each
pitch, and yaw, not like the aspect
dead ahead, and starboard,
that washes the sea and sky with the hush
of apparition--

Dusk now, it is clear.
At the horizon to the west
below spattered stars of early night,
before the glower of a sunset silent
as that flash at Kwajalein,
thunderheads in silhouette might be
far stands of cottonwoods

and these rolling swells wheat fields
blowing in an Iowa prairie night,
or rushes swaying
in the marshes of Mars.

ALRESFORD FORD

In East Anglia a towpath follows the left bank of the Colne River from
Wivenhoe to Brightlingsea. Midway on this path, Alresford Creek debouches into
the Colne. It must be crossed but is impassable except, by lore, upstream some
distance, at Alresford Ford. No one is quite sure where it is.

I could have drowned trying to ford
Alresford Ford,
or pronounce it.
Arlsferd Ford is how it is said,
a nice
      metathesis
like "butterfly" for "flutterby,"
lithely redundant
              and oxymoronic too.
As it happens it's
a mudded unmarked crossing
not fit at all for crossing.

WHAT IS IT OF A TREE

What is it of a tree
that a bird alights on it and not
another better
or, at least, equally formed
that arrests you too mid-
walk, mid-reverie, mid
animated colloquy within
so suddenly silenced?

THE CHANGING LIGHT OF SANDERLINGS

Two bucks and a doe browse near.
Ears flicker, tails flick, tongues lick between
their camel jaws mid-chew while they stare
emptily, each blank black eye
a preternatural indifference.
A fawn, still speckled, scampers ungainly
uphill toward a just-fledged crow
that flyhops six or eight yards away
in whatever direction whenever the fawn
draws too near until the fawn
crumples to rest too tired to wander
even to its mother's leaking teats.

Long-legged little girl thirty years ago
chased terns, curlews, willets and sandpipers
but mainly sanderlings, skittering
in a seeming imitation of them
into the spume of receding surf
until the next incoming wave's uprush
sent all in a scurry back upbeach, the birds
unruffled, my daughter drenched to above her knees
and flopping on her beach towel too tired even
to eat her lunch.

That girl, this fawn,
each only moments earlier
so sure of her part here.

CHIMERA

"He went like that," Spade said, "like a fist when you open your hand."
—Dashiell Hammett, *The Maltese Falcon*

What skitters there, silver, and
   now what are they, scampering, gray maybe
down the gutter by the curb across the street? --
   baby mice, or voles,
or moles running close
to the curb face to avoid the rise
 of the street to its crest   racing,
   overtaking, falling back,
         regaining ground and

 stopping now and again to gloat over a lead,
Or are they leaves blown, or sucked
through an unseen tunnel, a wind funnel?

Crossing the street you see they are leaves,
dry russet leaves,
borne down downstream on a rivulet
running from an overwatered lawn.

In this way—say, imagining a train
leaving a platform so smoothly the passengers
think the next train is moving—
Einstein divined relativity.
And so you draw closer, to examine
and see they aren't leaves at all,
and there is no water, is no gutter, [delete second *is*?]
no curb or kerb but nothing
at   actually
  all.

Now all there is for you to do
   is work out the proofs.

LATE FALL RUN
After Exxon Valdez

Land's End long
after summer's end
in tumbledown fall,
the swollen salmon sun
far at the end of the sea
slips under the edge of the world
where days roll in free-fall cataracts
like these crashing streams where we,
like salmon packed pectoral to pectoral, gill to gill,
are swimming almost spent upstream to spawn
in the gravel beds of our birth, our
ancestral redds, and suddenly wonder why.

In such a witless moment we lose purchase
in the water, are swept backwards in its torrents
down the coastal mountain creeks
ending our lives our lines, our race
in a crash on a boulder we had just swum past
on our way up.
Only old words hold
this gloaming, this darkling
cold wet stone world.

AFTER SOLSTICE

Made to wade this winter deep into March
to see the sun again, to hear robins
blurt their unsubtle Welsh-lilt palavers,
so more melodic, more pregnant than any,
than all of our poor tongues,

we wait to feel the ground beneath us stir,
to split for billions of greening god's heads to burst
like warheads fixed on Minuteman missiles
breaching their underground silos that in hours
rolling into crazed copper days will rise
as Queen Anne's Lace, and the wild iris shoots,

the starts of spring, though for now
the thunderheads of winter still rule
the skies, still grip the Fool
of Hearts.

VII.

War and Gardening

War is the normal occupation of man—war and gardening.
—Winston Churchill

BASIC TRAINING
Fort Ord, California, July 1968

Doc dead, struck dead
by the evening Del Monte Express twenty years ago
ended Steinbeck's stories of him.
Canneries shuttered, the sardine fleet scuttled,
even squid boats lie abandoned on the beach
or wheel with the tides at anchor
in the harbor just over
these spindrift dunes on Monterey Bay.

Drill Instructor Sergeant LaCour
orders twenty-five wind sprints
until you puke, yells
for twenty more then
for slobbery vomit fifteen more.
No *Hut, Hut,* but *Tet, Tet--*
Tet Tet Tet he screams.
No *Martin, Martin.* No *Robert,*
Robert.

Will sustains you until another will,
seeming to loom over your left shoulder
storms and overthrows your old order.
Your frame buckles, your grain of a mind and reed of a body
collapse in a blind white haze
or rather they determine to because
there was, it has always after seemed to you,
another wind sprint, another hundred yards
left in you.

In that same way, your new
very veteran platoon sergeant
explains weeks later as you puke seasick
over the transom rail of a troop ship steaming
into the South China Sea,
we decide to die.

VIETNAM MEMORIAL

Vietnam Veterans Memorial
is its proper name, though those words
are nowhere chiseled in its black granite,
only names of dead and lost, no names
of veterans.

Its low long walls meet
like blades of an iron ploughshare
that has ceased its harrowing and turning
and begun to sink in the Potomac bog.
The January sun is low, and so it lies
in the shadow of the Lincoln Memorial.
The Vietnam Memorial seems most fitting at dusk,
when closest soldiers can seem strangers.
I walk it the wrong way, from the end of the east wall
to where the two walls meet in a wide *v*.

French and Asian school children with ice creams,
adult tourists and more schoolchildren still,
amble between the wall and me the other direction,
jostle and pose for cameras
and occasionally are curious in English—

> *Isn't Billy Joe a funny name*
for a soldier?

It is maybe forty yards before my eyes alight
not on my reflected face, but a name,
one carved in the center of Panel 35 E.
It is my name. I walk on
to the beginning of the guided tour
where a book lists in rows and columns
as they had once dressed in formation,
as the gravestones align in Arlington
and Gettysburg, the dead and missing.
I find mine, and the name of my brother too;

his is cut in 56 E.
Each man was killed in 1968,
the year the North launched the Tet Offensive
that began to win the war for them,
the year, at home, of assassinations.

Marine Lance Corporal John Briscoe of Baltimore, Maryland,
was killed by enemy fire at Quang Tri January 26.

Army Sergeant Larry Briscoe of Denver, Colorado,
died in a firefight at Binh Dinh May 6.

Military records tell little more than this
and the fact each man was "negro."

Who were those men who took our places
in the ambushes and firefights
endlessly reprised, who took from us forever
the glory of this granite, these
spattered rounds of camera flashes, this parade
of ice cream cones and cotton candy
borne like torches by strangers going the other way
whose names may yet engrave
another war memorial.

RUNIT DOME

Who left among us
knows of Runit Island
on Enewetak Atoll
in the western Pacific west
of the main Marshall Islands?

A man from Tuman--no, it was Talofofo,
on Guam, was said to thin the thighbones
of some unknown one of his fighting cocks
so it would lose, and he had bet against it.

Who would choose,
who chose Enewetak site
for forty atomic bomb explosions?
Few would forget the name
if it were heard again.

The name of the man from Talofofo
was Porfirio, or Pancero or Pedro Palting.
All the cock fighters knew him and knew,
they thought, that he'd learned the occult procedure
from some master in Malaysia.
One man was sure one cock had been Enola,
and Little Boy another.

Four of Enewetak Atoll's forty islands
were vaporized by the forty blasts.
Runit Island was by lot chosen as the burial site
for the hissing, humming glowing atomic slag,

But none of them knew how to do
the occult procedure. In the Philippines
it is common, and passed down,
was all they ever said they knew.

Runit Dome entombs what atomic waste
can be contained in fifty-gallon drums,
poison enough for all the planets.
Its size is that of a sports stadium.
We will need more Runit Domes now.
It is cracking. And the sea here, where we
have overheated the earth, is rising.

Palting, is there thinning in your thighs?
Has someone slit them to shave your leg bones?
Ah, as you know, if the cock don't crow,
the sun won't rise.
So crow, Palting. Crow.

NATIVE, EXOTIC

Wild irises uphill
bloom in white or blue
depending on which side it seems
the canyon climbs, or falls,
lupine too, orange
bush monkey flower,
and wild blue indigo.

                    Here, downhill
bumblebees, honeybees and black
mason bees hum, buzz, bob
on stems, petals, and in
bee-circus aerobatics
in the very air that wreathes
the pollen-spattered petals
of very different flowers,
violet French lavender,
and orange South African
bulbine.

In his Giverny Monet would see
all this, and all else I miss.

FIRST CASUALTY
The Permanent Court of Arbitration, The Hague

Ethiopia stands in the dock
accused by Eritrea
of crimes against the laws of war.
Eritrea charges that during their two-years-long
deadly ground and more deadly air war waged
at the end of the millennium
Ethiopia bombed churches, mosques, and ports
among other sites having no
military value but the terror
of civilians. This is Eritrea's
gravest accusation.

In defense of this charge your main witness
is General Mohamad who oversaw
the planning and ordered
every Ethiopian air strike.
General Mohamad testifies for four days
that he knew and, warily, how he knew
that the power plant at Hirgigo,
the water reservoir in the Eritrean desert,
the Coptic churches, twelve mosques and the port
on the Red Sea all hid enemy weapons caches,
anti-aircraft batteries, and intelligence apparatus.
The Ethiopian command respected the lives
of the Eritrean people, he testified.
At all events, there was insufficient ordnance
to wage a campaign of civilian terror.

You have questioned him in English.
He has answered in his language, Amharic,
and also in Tigrinya, the language
of Eritrea. His testimony, his calm candor
draw no cross-examination from any
among Eritrea's battery of lawyers.
The French president of the Court declares
a brief recess and you walk with your witness

out of the majestic courtroom and down
the steps of the Peace Palace, the one other legacy
of the failed 1899 Peace Conference.
You shake hands. He leaves in a long black car.

You walk slowly back into the Palace, up
the grand staircase and down the corridor
thinking for the first time in days
of the delicate cease-fire that brings the parties here.
The heads of state were once closest of friends
and what is more friends in arms against the Soviet Derg.
These two poorest of countries on Earth,
once the kingdom of Abyssinia
then waged war against each other
killing more than a hundred thousand people.

Reentering the courtroom you re-fix on your case.
Eritrea will call the next witness
and you will cross-examine him.
You have prepared for him.
You think of Robert Jackson's inept questioning
of Hermann Göring at Nuremberg
then laugh to yourself, confident.
This witness will address the most minor of charges.
He is the Eritrean Embassy driver
who after the Ambassador and all other staff
had been expelled as *personae non gratae*
stayed on as the sole Embassy caretaker
in the Ethiopian capital, Addis Ababa.
He stands, is sworn, sits, and testifies
clear and composed as General Mohamad had
that in the fall of 1998
the Ethiopian police stopped his car,
struck him in the mouth with a pistol butt,
then took him manacled to the First Police Station
where he was held and sometimes beaten
for six months before he was turned over
to the Red Cross at the frontier.
None of that, you reflect, violates the laws of war

but at most the laws of diplomatic relations if,
of course, any of it is true.
Your client Ethiopia has all along denied
that anything of the sort had happened to this man.

You rise to cross-examine him.
Your client's agent hands you a note:

> *He says he was imprisoned at the First Police Station.*
> *He was imprisoned at the Third.*

UPRIVER

Repatriation of Remains

Up the Mekong they come still
fifty and sixty years on
by boat and oar, boat and motor,
by canoe and oar, by basket boat,
by lashed-bamboo rafts they pole like pirogues.
Some come from the Midwest
hard by the Missouri, or Mississippi,
some come from the East by the Ohio, or Allegheny.
Those from the Mississippi Delta
or Louisiana bayou
do best. They all come
to claim and recover remains
of fathers, husbands, uncles, and brothers
(no one comes for sons anymore)
who had been soldiers, sailors, airmen, marines,
long officially Missing in Action.
They come to change the records
to Killed in Action.

One old poet wrote it is sweet and right
to die for one's country.
To that emperor-pleasing sentiment
these people would say no,
but it is right to journey here, to go
into this hissing jungle, for this.
An older poet, beginning his story
with the Greek hero Achilles raging
on an Aegean beach over a slight
over a girl, and refusing to fight
later tells of the aged King of Troy
risking death to enter Achilles's camp
to beg for the body of his dead son Hector.
In all its tellings through all the centuries
Priam, King of Troy, in the end is dead
and Achilles too.

Old Priam, old
women at Golgotha,
and you old men and women
poling upriver into Indochina,
whyever do you bother?

John Briscoe, 2019

John Briscoe's poetry has been praised by *Foreword, Kirkus,* and *US Review of Books*, as well as others. He received the Oscar Lewis Award for Western History in 2020, among other awards, for his book *Crush: The Triumph of California Wine,* and for his other historical works. His book *A Child's Christmas in San Francisco*, a work of narrative and light verse, was a Foreword Indie Finalist in 2021.

Briscoe is also a lawyer, advising and representing clients such as Kuwait, Mexico, the Republic of Korea (South Korea), Ethiopia and the United Nations in cases of international-boundary disputes, the dumping of nuclear waste into the oceans, the environmental consequences of war, and alleged violations of the laws of war.

He is a Distinguished Fellow at the University of California, Berkeley School of Law, and has served on the Advisory Board of the St. Mary's College of California MFA Program in Creative Writing since its founding in 1995. Briscoe is co-owner of Sam's Grill, a famed gathering place of writers, artists, steamfitters, cops, poets and politicians in downtown San Francisco.

.

THE PAGE POETS SERIES

Number 12
The Public Sound by Marina Lazzara

Number 13
Record of Records by Rod Roland

Number 14
Strangers We Have Known by John Briscoe